Love? in New York

CALLIE'S JOURNAL

0,50

À lire progressivement en anglais !

Tip Tongue Journal, c'est un carnet de voyage linguistique palpitant

Les héros, jeunes Français comme le lecteur, racontent et dessinent leurs aventures avec des amis anglophones dans un journal de bord, qu'ils s'efforcent de rédiger progressivement dans la langue de Shakespeare (le dernier chapitre est à 100% en anglais).

Avec Tip Tongue Journal, lire et écrire de l'anglais devient naturel

Pas besoin de dictionnaire, les héros font tout le boulot. Un plaisir de lecture immense, la fierté de comprendre une langue étrangère, et une incitation à écrire, se raconter, dessiner, comme le font les personnages, et ainsi mémoriser plus et mieux.

Avec Tip Tongue Journal, on découvre les vertus du crayon et du stylo !

Dans leur journal, les héros prennent leurs crayons et leurs stylos pour explorer la langue et la mémoriser à leur manière. Ils utilisent sans le savoir des méthodes de mémorisation et de créativité : *sketchnoting, doodle, bullet journal*... C'est amusant, et efficace !

L'audio-book

Tout comme dans la collection de romans **Tip Tongue**, chaque titre offre une version intégrale audio téléchargeable. Un véritable bain de langue pour découvrir comment se prononce un mot en langue étrangère au moment où on le lit.

Pour découvrir la collection, accéder aux audio-books et aux ressources pédagogiques :
https://tip-tongue-anglais.syros.fr/
Ou téléchargez l'appli **Syros Live** et flashez les couvertures.

La collection des romans Tip Tongue se décline en anglais, espagnol, allemand, et pour tous les âges de 8 à 16 ans et plus !
Elle a obtenu en 2015 le **Label européen des langues**, récompensant l'excellence en matière d'apprentissage innovant. Chaque titre correspond à un niveau cible du CECRL (Cadre européen commun de référence pour les langues), sur lequel sont basés les programmes scolaires.

Pour choisir son Tip Tongue

- / 8-10 ans / CE2-CM1-CM2 / A1 Introductif
- / 10-12 ans / CM2-6e-5e / A1 Découverte
- / 12-14 ans / 5e-4e-3e / A2 Intermédiaire
- / 14-16+ ans / 3e-2nde-1re / B1 Seuil

**TIP TONGUE, C'EST TOUT UN PROGRAMME :
PLAISIR, CURIOSITÉ, CONFIANCE EN SOI, RÉUSSITE !**

Tip Tongue JOURNAL

Une collection dirigée par Stéphanie Benson

Label européen des langues

ISBN : 978-2-74-852470-3

25, avenue Pierre-de-Coubertin, 75013 Paris
Loi n° 49-956 du 16 juillet 1949
sur les publications destinées à la jeunesse,
modifiée par la loi n° 2011-525 du 17 mai 2011.

N°éditeur: 10237759 - Dépôt légal: février 2019

Love? in New York

CALLIE'S JOURNAL

Stéphanie Benson

illustrations de Juliette Maroni

SYROS

KEEP OUT

DO NOT READ

PRIVATE PROPERTY

GO AWAY

CLOSE THIS JOURNAL IMMEDIATELY!

GET LOST!

GET OUT OF MY INTIMACY!

THIS JOURNAL
(diary, notebook, thing)

BELONGS TO:

Callie @Kali (Caroline) Normand

DOB:*
23rd October

Age:
nearly 18

Address:
12 Jones Street,
New York, USA

Favorite things in life:

Graphic Design
(why I'm in New York)

Bob Dylan
(discovered ten months ago, now I'm a total fan)

Allen Gardner
(it's a secret, he doesn't know... yet)

Visiting art museums

Eating hamburgers

Reading poetry

Appearance:
5 ft 6 (1 m 56 approximately), shoulder length brown hair, green eyes, big ears

* Date of birth

MONDAY 27TH AUGUST

Today is a beautiful day because I'm on a plane flying to New York. Here, above the clouds, over the Atlantic Ocean, it's warm and sunny. My heart is warm and sunny because I'm going to New York to study Graphic Design.

Where?

At the New York School for Visual Arts!

NYSVA Here I Come!!! I'm coming! I'm on my way!

J'arrive !

So... OK, let's go!

BACK TO NYC

Retour à New York

« To LEARN, YOU MUST PRACTICE »

ou (in French) : pour apprendre il faut pratiquer.

C'est l'une des phrases préférées de mon amie (même si elle a 70 ans) Sue Ann Vandenberg.

So I'm practicing English because I want to learn really good English. AND according to Sue Ann writing a journal every day is a very good way to practice. One page minimum per day and in one year my English will be perfect. More or less. AND ma mère a ajouté son grain de sel...

J'ai rencontré *Sue Ann* en novembre dernier quand je suis venue pour la première fois à New York. Elle est super riche et collectionneuse d'art contemporain.

Maman

Toi qui adores dessiner, tu n'as qu'à intégrer les phrases que tu veux apprendre dans un dessin. Comme ça tu les mémoriseras mieux !

(toujours dans l'avion)

I'M STILL ON THE PLANE TO NEW YORK → **BECAUSE… FLIGHT TIME = 6 HOURS!!!**

→ **SO… LET'S WRITE IN ENGLISH** *(pour faire passer le temps)*

FLASHBACK:

10 months AGO → IL Y A dix mois

Maman

Et si on te trouvait un séjour dans un pays anglophone pour préparer l'oral d'anglais au bac ?

Cool ! Où ça ?

Moi

Voyons… J'ai une super collègue américaine avec qui je m'entends bien : Diana Gardner. Elle habite New York…

RÉSULTAT DES COURSES...
RESULT OF THE SHOPPING ???*

My Top Ten Favorite Moments

1. Living for ten days in Manhattan, New York City
2. Discovering Greenwich Village → *Se prononce* GREN-itch
3. Baby-sitting Dylan Gardner

mes top rencontres ♥

4. Meeting Allen Gardner (Dylan's brother)
5. Meeting Sue Ann Vandenberg (age 70, art collector)
6. **SPEAKING ENGLISH ALL THE TIME**

* *Après vérification, on ne peut pas traduire les expressions littéralement.*

courses = shopping OU races (= sport)

10 jours magiques passés à New York !* Et envie d'y retourner le plus vite possible. Puis, 3 mois plus tard, Frank (le mari de la collègue de ma mère et le père de Dylan et Allen) m'a envoyé un lien pour découvrir l'école dont je rêvais, la NYSVA, j'ai regardé...

C'est là que Papa intervient :

Papa

Yeah. Wonderful. Great idea.

HOW MUCH DOES IT COST???

Dad's favorite question

HOW MUCH does it cost? (ça coûte combien ?)

HOW MANY years does it last? (ça dure combien d'années ?)

HOW LONG before you're financially independent? (ça prendra combien de temps avant que tu sois financièrement indépendante ?)

Dad's favorite phrase

You should start thinking about being

FINANCIALLY INDEPENDENT

(il me répète ça depuis que j'ai dix ans)

*À lire dans le roman Tip Tongue *Dylan Dilemma*

Moi, l'autonomie financière, je veux bien. Mais à 10 ans ? Sans diplômes ??

Papa est un SELF-MADE MAN. Les Américains l'adoreraient. Au collège, il lavait les voitures des voisins pour gagner son argent de poche ; au lycée, il travaillait le samedi dans un fast-food ; à l'université, il livrait des pizzas et donnait des cours de maths aux petits pour financer ses cours d'anglais...

And now, he teaches maths IN ENGLISH!

Bref, j'évoque la question financière auprès des Gardner (les parents de Dylan) et voici leur proposition...

DYLAN'S PARENTS' PROPOSAL:

A) Callie can stay with us (so she doesn't need to rent a room).
B) Callie can help with Dylan (not baby-sit, teenage-sit).
C) Callie will have meals with us (so she doesn't need money for food).
D) We give Callie $50 a week pocket money.

PERFECT!!!

BUT HOWEVER
UNFORTUNATELY UNHAPPILY

Dad

This NewYorkSchool ofVisualArts HOW MUCH?

Me

What do you mean, how much? It's a school.

Callie... This is America...
This is a Private School...
In America schools COST MONEY.

HOW MUCH DOES IT COST?

We look on the website

TWENTY THOUSAND DOLLARS PER SEMESTER → **HEART ATTACK**

J'écris la somme en lettres parce que ça fait moins mal

WHAT ??????

60 000!!!!!!!!!!

That's SIXTY THOUSAND DOLLARS a year!!! That's IMPOSSIBLE Callie! We don't have that much money! I'm sorry but WE CAN'T PAY FOR THIS SCHOOL!

J'ai bien cru que Papa allait s'étouffer → *(Dad choking, can't breathe)*

Je le fais court, mais Papa a passé beaucoup de temps à me dire que nous n'avions pas autant d'argent et a décliné en plein de couleurs le fait qu'il ne pouvait pas financer cette école... jusqu'à ce qu'un mail de Frank Gardner, qui tombait à pic, évoque la solution à l'américaine du STUDENT LOAN ou prêt étudiant.

STUDENT LOAN

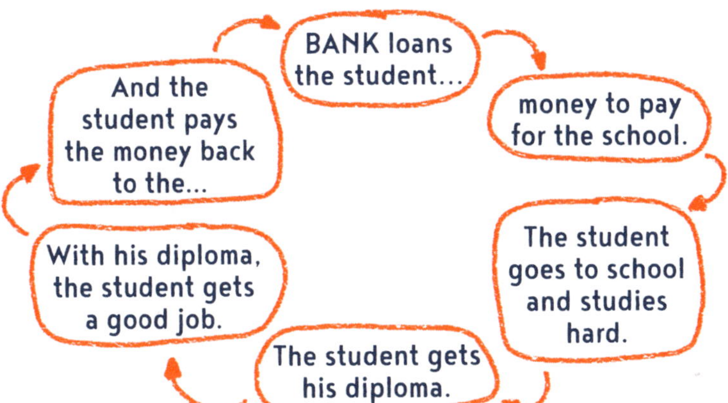

LATER

ON THE PLANE STILL OVER THE ATLANTIC...

Ça devient compliqué de se repérer dans le temps quand on traverse différentes zones temporelles. Je crois que j'ai dormi. IN ENGLISH!

I think I slept. → **Passé composé FR (action finie) =** *Prétérit USA*

I must remember

EXEMPLES :

j'ai dormi = I slept

j'ai adoré New York = I loved New York

j'ai rencontré plein de gens = I met lots of people

je me suis amusée = I had fun

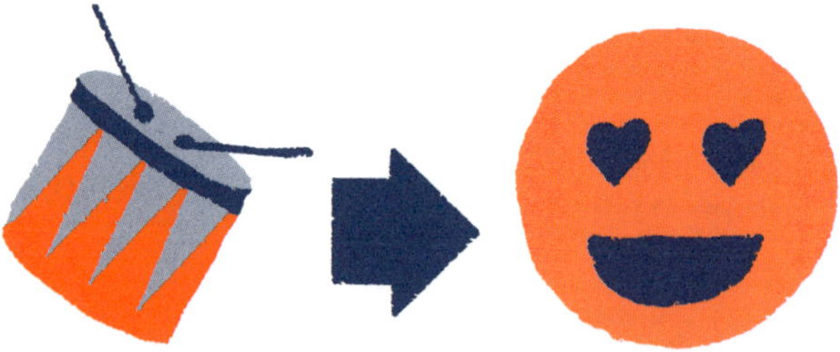

ET.... *(roulement de tambour)*...

j'ai rencontré quelqu'un de particulier = I met someone special.

J'ai mangé = I ate (for lunch I think) today:

Lasagne and Salad, Apple Pie and Cheese.

The air hostess told me:

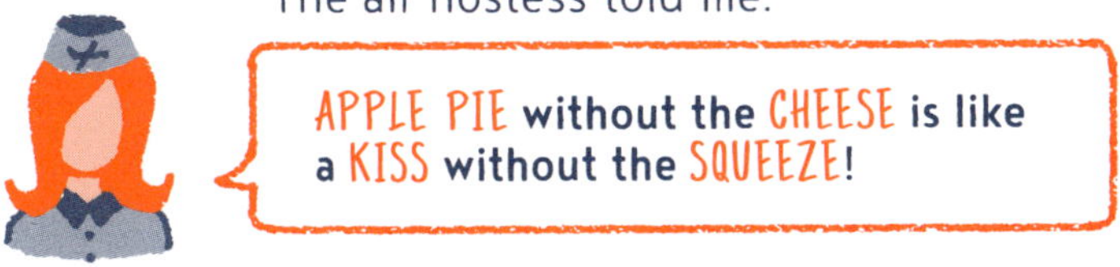

USA
Apple Pie + cheese

VS

FRANCE
Quince jelly + cheese
eh oui, « coing » c'est « quince »

CONCLUSION :

Les Américains n'aiment pas faire un baiser sans prendre l'autre dans leurs bras, et ils mangent la tarte aux pommes avec du fromage... (Cela dit, moi, j'aime bien le fromage avec la pâte de coings).

BACK TO THE FLASHBACK

Bref, une fois réglée la question financière (à la satisfaction de papa qui trouve que c'est une excellente idée de responsabiliser les jeunes quant à leur formation), il ne restait que celle de la sélection à l'entrée de l'école. Parce qu'en plus ils ne prennent pas tout le monde !

TO GET INTO THE NEW YORK SCHOOL OF VISUAL ARTS

FIRSTLY → you must complete the application form

SECONDLY → you must write a cover letter explaining in detail your motivation

C'est la traditionnelle lettre de motivation...

THIRDLY → you must attach a portfolio (scanned colour photos of your work)*

FOURTHLY → you must submit a scholarship application**

To apply = postuler

* J'ai envoyé les photos du dossier que j'ai présenté à l'option Arts plastiques au bac.

** Les bourses aux USA sont accordées en fonction de ton travail, pas en fonction du revenu de tes parents !

Nous avons passé une semaine à constituer le dossier.
Puis nous l'avons envoyé par mail.
Puis nous avons attendu.

In English, **REMEMBER:**

Past action finished and done = simple past tense...

So...

We SPENT a week doing the application file.
Then we SENT it by email.
Then we WAITED.

THEN, FIVE WEEKS LATER, WE RECEIVED THE ANSWER...

Dear Caroline*,
We received and processed your application to our BFA** in Graphic Design, and are delighted to inform you that you have been accepted for the first year beginning September 3rd.

New York School of Visual Arts
1090 Upper 23rd Street
New York City

MY REACTION... SEE NEXT PAGE.

* The Americans ALWAYS use your first name.

** Bachelor of Fine Arts, l'équivalent de la licence arts plastiques ou du diplôme des beaux-arts.

ME GOING COMPLETELY MAD

- I'm going to have a new life in New York!
- I immediately sent an email to Frank and Diana, to Dylan, to Sue Ann and to ♥ Allen.

MY EMAIL:
THE SCHOOL SAID YES!!!

PEOPLE	REPLIES TO MY EMAIL
Frank 	I knew you could do it!!! Can't wait to see U again.
Diana 	Congratulations!! So happy for you!
Dylan 	That's so cool. My favorite babysitter is coming to stay!
Sue Ann 	Wonderful! When do you arrive? *Elle s'est portée garante pour mon prêt étudiant. Je lui dois tellement !*
Allen 	Good. *J'avoue que je m'attendais à un peu plus d'enthousiasme. I'm a bit sad, a bit disappointed...*

ANNOUNCEMENT: This is the pilot speaking. We're beginning our approach to the JFK airport in New York, so would you please return to your seats and fasten your seat-belts... **I'M SOOO EXCITED!!!**

Diana, Frank and Dylan came to meet me at the airport with a banner!

But WHAT DOES DYLAN WANT TO TELL ME?? *Mystery...*

AT HOME IN MY ROOM AT THE GARDNERS'

SKETCH OF MY ROOM

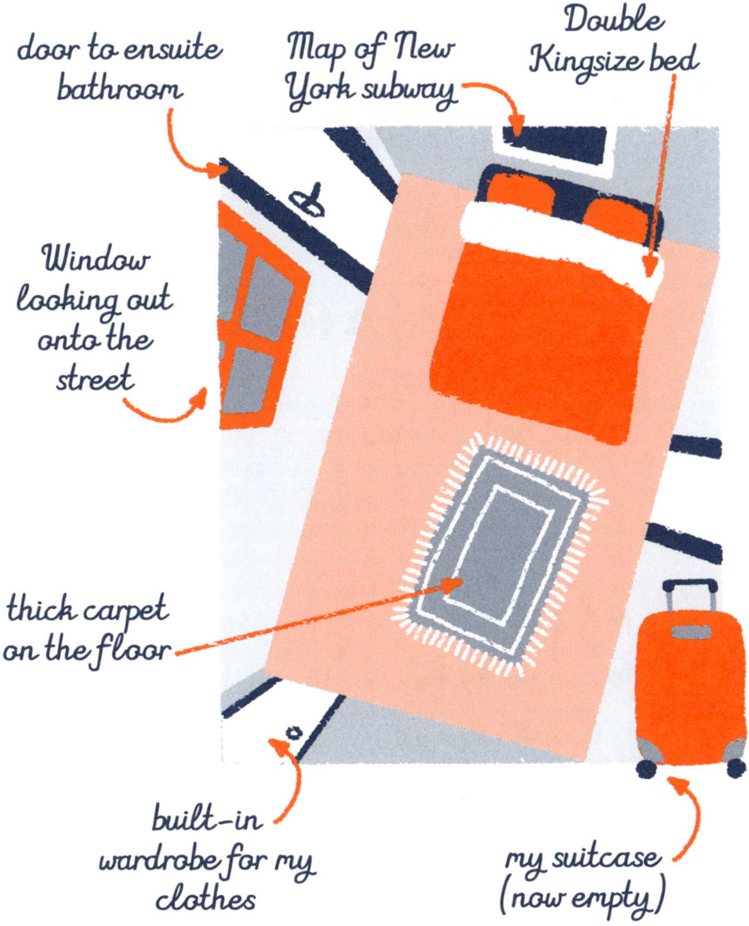

LATE EVENING

Back from the restaurant

WELL THAT WAS A SLAP IN THE FACE

DON'T CRY CALLIE

HE'S NOT WORTH IT, DEAR

I'M SO SAD

I'M SO DISAPPOINTED

Je me dis que si je raconte la soirée en anglais ça fera moins mal, mais je n'en suis pas certaine. J'ai la gorge serrée, une boule dans le ventre, et envie de tuer quelqu'un.

I WANT TO KILL HIM/HER THEM

OK, Callie, just tell the story

Dialogue entre moi et moi-même

EARLIER

B4 the restaurant *(before = B4 = Avant)*

Frank: Hey, Callie, we thought for your first evening back in the village, we'd do a burger.

Diana: Yeah, like last time when you arrived. We've invited Sue Ann.

Frank: And Allen, of course.

Dylan: Callie, I have to tell you something.

Frank: Are you ready, Callie, or do you need to change, take a shower?

Me: No, I'm fine, we can go...

(Thinking I'm going to see Allen...)

Diana: OK then, let's go.

DINNER AT THE MINETTA TAVERN

113 MacDougal Street

First, a girl with a badge saying LIZZIE accompanied us to a table.

Pendant qu'on attendait Sue Ann et Allen, j'ai fait des croquis. Les murs de la Minetta Tavern, qui se dit ‹‹ French style bistrot ››, sont recouverts de dessins des clients célèbres du restaurant.
C'est un endroit génial.

Eugene O'Neill
(playwright)

Ernest Hemingway
(writer)

Ezra Pound
(poet)

E. E. Cummings
(poet)

Dylan Thomas
(another poet)

Joe Gould
(author of the longest book ever written and aka* Professor Seagull – aussi connu comme professeur Mouette)

The Minetta Tavern is an amazing place.

Frank said this restaurant has served food and drink (probably more drink than food) to so many famous artists.

* aka = also known as

Then Sue Ann arrived. Sue Ann and Diana are now really good friends.Depuis que Sue Ann a aidé Frank et Diana à retrouver leur fils*, ils sont devenus très proches. Logique. Et pour l'instant aucun de nous ne se doute de rien... Nous attendons, et pas de Allen...

Frank

Well, let's order, shall we?
We're not going to wait all night.

Allen's an artist. Artists are always late.

Sue Ann

Frank

Fine, but I'm hungry. Let's order.
Waitress! We'll order now please.

Moi, je regarde Dylan. Il me fixe d'un air bizarre. I say:

Are you OK?

Me

He nods, but he looks unhappy.

*voir le roman Tip Tongue *Dylan Dilemma*

The Menu

ENTRÉES

MOULES FRITES .... 28$
Maine bouchot mussels, white wine, shallots, parsley, pommes frites

MONKFISH ROASTED ON THE BONE .... 40$
Champignons de Paris, bacon lardon, fingerling potato, bordelaise

FILET OF TROUT MEUNIÈRE .... 33$
with jumbo lump crabmeat and brioche croutons

PASTA ZA ZA .... 24$
fresh pasta with pancetta, sage, Parmesan, and a fried egg

ROASTED FREE-RANGE CHICKEN .... 34$
with Swiss chard and pommes aligot

LONG ISLAND DUCK BREAST .... 39$
mandarin orange, caramelized endive, parsnip puree, sauce bigarade

MINETTA BURGER .... 25$
with cheddar, caramelized onions and pommes frites

BLACK LABEL BURGER .... 33$
selection of prime dry-aged beef cuts
with caramelized onions and pommes frites

STEAK FRITES .... 38$
with maître d'hôtel butter or sauce béarnaise

(Entrée is main course, Hors d'œuvre is entrée)

OUR ORDER

Two Steak Frites
Dylan and me

Two Filets of Trout
Sue Ann and Diana

Long Island Duck Breast
Frank

= meilleures amies du monde

Nos repas arrivent et nous sommes en train de manger quand, soudain... En fait, je me dis rétrospectivement que j'aurais dû comprendre. Quand je fais la liste des indices :

CLUES I SHOULD HAVE UNDERSTOOD

1. Allen's really short response to my email saying I was coming to New York
2. Allen's absence at the airport
3. Dylan looking unhappy
4. Dylan saying he has to talk to me about something
5. Allen being late for the restaurant

CONCLUSION:
NEVER
EVER
TRUST BOY FRIENDS

Ne jamais faire confiance

THE SCENE

The five of us really enjoying our meal. Dylan arriving with this really weird (= strange) girl.

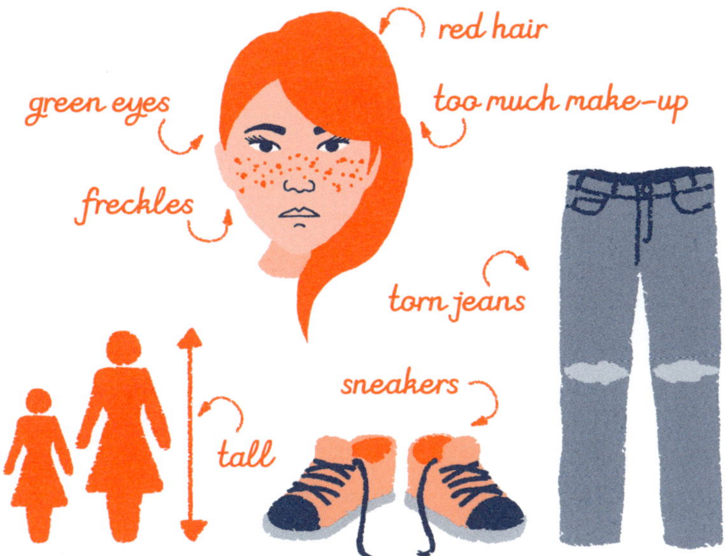

Hi Everyone! This is Cilla. We're getting married!

Nobody speaks. After a minute or two of silence, Allen says:

Got to go! See you around!

And they leave.

Je ne me suis JAMAIS sentie aussi **HUMILIATED**

REACTIONS

1. Stupified Silence. → Everybody together
2. Well, that's a surprise. I need a drink. → Sue Ann
3. Don't cry, Callie. He's not worth* it. → Dylan whispering to me
4. He's got to be joking! → Frank

MY FEELINGS

I FEEL SO TOTALLY...

SHOCKED HUMILIATED ANGRY
DISAPPOINTED BETRAYED UNHAPPY
STUPID SAD FURIOUS

I WANT TO...

SCREAM RUN BACK TO FRANCE
TALK TO MY FRIENDS CRY
JETER MON VERRE POUR LE VOIR SE BRISER EN MILLE MORCEAUX CONTRE LE MUR

* Worth = Value = il n'en vaut pas la peine (mouais...)

Et maintenant, je n'arrive pas à dormir.

I CAN'T SLEEP.

Je me dis que j'ai été idiote de croire que j'allais arriver à New York et qu'Allen allait me faire une déclaration d'amour éternel alors qu'on se connaît à peine.

I THOUGHT HE LOVED ME.
BECAUSE I LOVED HIM.

Enfin, ç'aurait pu être pire.
Oh YES? How?

(Ceci est une conversation silencieuse entre Callie la Française et American Callie.)

J'aurais pu en parler à mes parents.
Right. You could have told HIS parents too.
J'aurais pu en parler à Sue Ann.
Only my French girl friends know.
Seulement mes copines françaises et...

DYLAN. I didn't tell him anything...
mais il a tout deviné. Il a essayé de me prévenir.
Yeah. He tried to warn me but it was TOO LATE.

THANK YOU, DYLAN.
YOU'RE MY FRIEND.

TUESDAY 28TH AUGUST

THE SHOW MUST GO ON

J'ai dû finir par m'endormir, parce que ce matin je me suis réveillée, et je me sentais mieux. Et j'ai pris des **RÉSOLUTIONS.**

CALLIE'S NEW YORK RESOLUTIONS

C'est un jeu de mots à partir de NEW YEAR RESOLUTIONS.

Je fais même des blagues en anglais !

I refuse to suffer for a boy who's « not worth it » as Dylan said.

I am a positive person. I am in New York. I refuse to be sad.

I am starting school to become a graphic designer. I need GOOD ENERGY.

I made a smoothie from: pineapple, banana, blueberry. I put the ingredients in the blender and imagined they were Allen. Then I drank the smoothie.

Dylan and I are going to visit my new school!

NYSVA HERE I COME!!!

BACK HOME, THE EVENING

J'ai tellement de trucs à raconter, je ne sais pas par où commencer...

JUST TELL THE STORY, CALLIE...

D'accord. Voilà. L'école est à 15 minutes de la maison.
Oops: The school is a fifteen minute walk from home.
(Frank said: it's perfectly situated, really close to us.)
The weather is beautiful. Warm and sunny with a soft breeze (Dylan said this).
Dylan is happy because I'm not sad (mais il ne voit pas toutes les larmes intérieures que je verse). He says he doesn't like Allen's girlfriend because:

1. **She's a groupie**
2. **She doesn't smile**
3. **She only wants Allen to be with her, not with his family and friends**

I asked: What does groupie mean?
Dylan said: It's like a rock star who has groupies that follow him around and think he's wonderful just because he's famous.
But Allen's not famous, I said.
No, but Cilla thinks he will be a famous artist and that's all she's interested in.

The NYSVA is on East 23rd Street. Il y a deux entrées avec au-dessus des portes un immense panneau comme ceci :

NEW YORK SCHOOL OF VISUAL ARTS

Dylan's reaction:

Ma convocation disait que je devais venir à 10 heures pour ‹‹ a general tour of the school, meet staff, teachers and second year students who'll show you the ropes ››. Dylan m'avait rassurée, on n'allait pas me montrer des cordes. C'était une métaphore probablement marine pour désigner le fonctionnement d'un établissement quelconque, les habitudes, comment on doit se comporter, etc... Je savais donc que j'allais rencontrer le personnel, les enseignants, les étudiants de deuxième année...

On avait à peine franchi le seuil qu'une fille mince aux cheveux noirs et courts qui me semblait vaguement familière s'est dirigée vers nous en demandant :

Freshman?*

Yes, said Dylan. Well her, not me. I'm a bit young. She's French.

La fille a souri.

I'm Lizzie. I'll take you on the grand tour before the meeting. Where you guys from?

J'ai ouvert la bouche pour répondre, mais le temps que je rassemble mes idées, Dylan a été plus rapide.

Actually, I'm from New York. But Callie's from that place in France where they make champagne.

Lizzie était sur le point de dire autre chose lorsque Dylan a ajouté :

Hey, I know you! You were working at the Minetta Tavern last night!

* Un homme tout frais qui vient d'arriver, ou un nouveau, quoi.

LIZZIE'S STORY

Ceci est un RÉSUMÉ. L'histoire originale était BEAUCOUP plus longue !

Yeah, well, you know, my folks (= my parents) have got money, but this is my life, my future, my choice, and I didn't want to ask them to pay for school, so I got a student loan at the bank, but at the same time, I started working evenings at the Tavern, because, you know, it's cool and the people are great and the pay's good, and you get a meal too, and yeah, sometimes I'm a bit tired, but, you know, I'm young, and if you want something you have to work for it, and I know this is THE best school EVER, so, you know, I think it's worth it!

Contrairement à Allen, qui, lui, n'en vaut pas la peine

Et lorsque Lizzie s'est enfin arrêtée de raconter son histoire, elle a commencé à me poser tout un tas de questions. Je les note ici pour apprendre les réponses pour une prochaine fois. Voici celles dont je me souviens :

LIZZIE'S QUESTIONS

HER QUESTIONS	MY ANSWERS
Where's that place you're from in France?	Reims. It's where champagne comes from.
What BFA are you doing?	Graphic Design.
What sort of career are you looking at?	I want to work in social or health advertising.
Why did you choose this school?	His dad found it for me (pointing at Dylan).
What's your portfolio about?	It's a project on Street Art and Advertising. I did it for my English exam in France.

FIRST IMPRESSIONS OF THE NEW YORK SCHOOL OF VISUAL ARTS

IT'S SO CLEAN!

THERE ARE FANTASTIC PICTURES EVERYWHERE. IT'S JUST AMAZING!

THE PEOPLE HERE ARE SO FRIENDLY!

IT BUZZES WITH CREATIVE VIBES

IT'S VERY RELAXED!

THERE ARE PEOPLE EVERYWHERE!

THE TEACHERS ARE SO COOL

THE COMPUTERS ARE ABSOLUTELY STATE OF THE ART

Lizzie said this (and ‹‹ state of the art ›› means dernier cri, nec plus ultra)

THERE'S A COFFEE SHOP!

LIZZIE TALKS ALL THE TIME

Dylan said this

YOU CALL THE TEACHERS BY THEIR FIRST NAME!

Puis nous sommes passés dans un bureau chercher mon emploi du temps. Les secrétaires étaient toutes super gentilles et détendues et m'ont souhaité la bienvenue.

THIS IS MY GENERAL SCHEDULE

Monday	Tuesday	Wednesday	Thursday	Friday
am	am	am	am	am
English literature	Computer Science	Art History	Design as Business	Space and Territory
Social Sciences	The Science of Colour	Aesthetics	Commerce	
pm	pm	pm	pm	pm
Studio work - Sketching	Studio work - Coloring	Studio work - Communi-cation	Studio work - motion graphics	Studio work - Photography

Then we went into this big lecture (= conférence) hall to meet all the teachers. Pendant que les enseignants se présentaient, j'ai croqué leur portrait.

Greg Lipsky

English teacher

Dark hair

Dark skin

Dark eyes

Passionate smile (he loves his subject)

American

Marina Sørensen

Danish

Teaches sketching

Red hair

Is watching me sketch her

Green eyes

Smiled at me

Daisy Najafi

Teaches color science and workshop

Part native Indian?

Long black hair

Smiley eyes (Dylan says)

Siru Qian

Motion graphics teacher

Chinese

Dyed (colored) blue hair

Glasses

Funny smile

Soft voice

Herb Henry

Sociology teacher

Tall

No hair (bald!)

Long nose

Not very well shaved

VERY thin ≠ fat

British

Rachel Tan

Economics teacher

Half Chinese

Short black hair

Earrings

Nose ring

Pierced upper lip

VERY serious

Ahmed El Khaffafi

Egyptian

Computer Science teacher

Dark hair

Salt and pepper beard

Shirt and tie

Serious

Jessica Walsh

British

Communications teacher

Blond hair

Blue eyes

Really pretty

Talks so fast!!!

Stefan Sagmeister

Geography (space and territory)

Austrian

Very blond hair

Funny accent

(I can understand everything!!)

Richard Wilde

Design as business teacher

Afro-American

BIG smile

Sparkling eyes

À midi, j'étais déjà épuisée. Lizzie (qui est restée avec nous) a suggéré qu'on aille boire un jus de fruits au coffee shop. Dylan (qui devait avoir faim mais qui n'a rien dit) a tout de suite adhéré à l'idée. Et donc, Lizzie a parlé. Et parlé. Et parlé. Je ne me souviens pas de tout, je crois que par moments j'ai décroché, mais bon, voici l'essentiel de ses explications :

LIZZIE'S EXPLANATIONS

At NYSVA (pronounced Niesvar) we don't really stop to eat a meal at lunch time. Maybe we have a quick coffee and a snack, maybe a sandwich, but that's all. We usually just work straight through till five... which is when I go to work.

Jusque-là, j'ai suivi. Une pause déjeuner qui est en fait une pause-café et Lizzie qui enchaîne avec son travail... Quel courage!

NOTE TO MYSELF: **EAT BREAKFAST!**

So as we stop at five, you'll have time to see exhibitions, movies, go to galleries. It's important to know what's going on in town. *What's going on*, you know, the Marvin Gaye song?

Bon apparemment, il y a une chanson de Marvin Gaye qui parle de ce qui est en train de se passer.

Right, so now you must buy all your stuff. Here's the list. Make sure you've got everything for Monday.

And this is your swipe card for the coffee shop and to get 10% off for your stuff. And your computer logins are written here on the card. And your card is also a discount card for exhibitions. You get half price off the entry charge.

Là, je suis sûre que j'ai décroché parce que je ne me souviens pas du reste. J'ai commencé à regarder la liste de fournitures qu'il fallait acheter. Et j'ai dit à Lizzie : ‹‹ I think I need to go and buy my stuff now.›› Elle ne nous a laissés partir que quand elle a vérifié que j'avais bien noté son numéro de téléphone ‹‹ just in case ››.

au cas où

Avec Dylan, on est donc partis vers ce qui est, selon lui, « the best shop in New York for all this kind of stuff ». C'était tellement bien de juste marcher en silence ! Lizzie est super gentille, mais qu'est-ce qu'elle est bavarde ! Bref.

VOICI TOUTE LA LISTE DE CE QUE J'AI ACHETÉ AUJOURD'HUI :

Stuff I needed to buy		DONE
Sketch pads (4)		☑
Watercolor pads (4)	aquarelle	☑
Note pads (4)		☑
Pencils (lead and color)	crayons papier	☑
Rulers and measuring stuff		☑
Color felt pens and biros	feutres / stylos bille	☑
Digital camera with memory cards		☐
USB sticks to save work in progress		☐
Watercolor paints		☑
Colored inks	encres	☑

Dylan avait raison. The shop was so cool. J'aurais pu y rester tout l'après-midi. Mais soudain, j'ai entendu :

Oh, hi Dylan! Surprise! So... This must be the French Au Pair Allen told me about. Does she speak English?

Cilla. Je n'en revenais pas. Elle m'a totalement ignorée, comme si je n'étais pas un vrai être humain, juste un chien en laisse ou un truc comme ça... Et puis, je n'étais pas une fille Au Pair. J'étais une étudiante et amie de la famille ! Zut !

I'm not an Au Pair. I'm a student and a friend of the family.

Yeah. And you look after Dylan in exchange for food and board. I call that an Au Pair, Frenchie. Bye Dylan!

Et elle est partie.

I HATE THIS GIRL!

Juste en y repensant, je suis absolument furieuse.

I AM SO FURIOUS !

DYLAN'S ADVICE:

« Don't listen to her »

« Don't let it bug you »

« Don't pay attention to her »

« She's only jealous because you're so FRENCH »

« I'm sure Allen didn't say you were an Au Pair »

« Let's go get an ice-cream »

Mais bon, je vais écouter Dylan et ne pas l'écouter, elle, ne pas la laisser m'atteindre, ne pas y faire attention (la glace était super bonne !). Sauf que je suis quand même furieuse.

OK. En cas de colère, il faut essayer d'analyser ce que l'on ressent.

WHY AM I SO FURIOUS???

A)

Because she's despising me (elle me méprise) and I can't defend myself in English (et je ne peux pas me défendre en anglais).

B)

Because Allen told her I was The Au Pair.

OK, but... Firstly, Au Pairs are nice people too. Au Pair is not an insult. Il faut vraiment que je me débarrasse de cette colère. Dylan, comme toujours, a été super mignon. Pendant qu'on mangeait nos glaces, il a tenté de me distraire :

Hey ! Let's go see a museum tomorrow. What's the museum you've always dreamed of visiting in New York?

So, tomorrow we'll visit the Whitney museum in the morning and the Guggenheim in the afternoon. Cool...

LATER

Hey, Callie, I was thinking. Why don't we invite Lizzie to come to the museums with us tomorrow?

Dylan planté à l'entrée de ma chambre

POURQUOI PAS, EN EFFET ?

I'll send her a text message.

Me

Yeah. Tell her we'll meet her outside the entrance at ten.

Dylan

Outside = dehors, donc DEVANT l'entrée

THIS IS WHAT I WILL TEXT TO LIZZIE:

Hi Lizzie, it's Callie. You gave me a visit of the NYSVA this morning. Tomorrow, I'm going to the Whitney museum and then to the Guggenheim. Want to come? Meet me outside the Whitney at ten (Dylan's coming too). Callie.

And maybe now I can go to sleep...

WEDNESDAY 29TH AUGUST

MORNING

WONDERFUL WEATHER

I ♥ NYC

I'm happy

I'm HUNGRY

I'm in NEW YORK

I'm not angry

woke up at seven
BREAKFAST
with Dylan

Fruit

Coffee

Cereals

Yoghurt

Pancakes with maple syrup

I WILL NOT LET CILLA BUG ME

J'ai toujours cru (je crois) au pouvoir de la pensée positive. Aujourd'hui, je tente l'écriture positive.

In English!

I'm a positive person!

Think positive!

Be Generous!

SMILE!

BE HAPPY!

Have fun!

ALWAYS HAPPY NOT SAD!!!

RECAP

EVENING

I've been walking ALL DAY

and I've been listening to Lizzie all day.

I'm exhausted Very tired

THE WHITNEY MUSEUM OF AMERICAN ART

At ten, outside the entrance, Lizzie was waiting. She started talking IMMEDIATELY!

Hi Guys! This is so cool! What a great idea, Callie...

I just love this museum, you know, it's amazing!

Before, it was on Madison avenue, but I really prefer this place, it's so much bigger

and... I don't know... it just feels so much better...

Et on n'avait même pas commencé à s'approcher de l'entrée !

Une fois devant les œuvres d'art, Lizzie s'est transformée. Elle s'est mise à parler clairement et lentement, en vérifiant que je puisse comprendre. C'était absolument génial, on avait l'impression d'avoir une guide pour nous tout seuls.

Then she turned to Dylan.

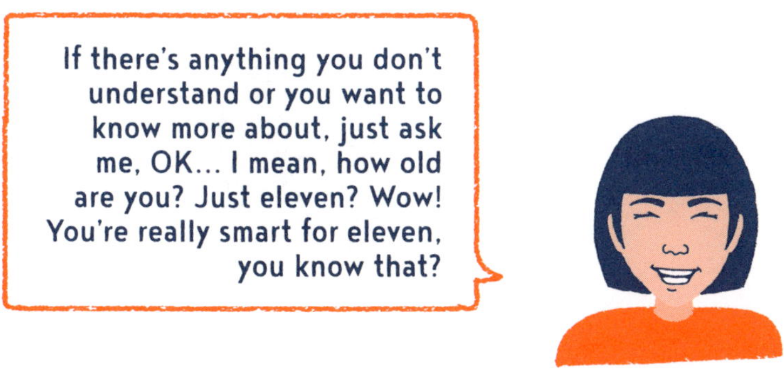

Lizzie, c'est évident, connaît son sujet sur le bout des doigts.

ELLE NOUS MONTRE :

EDWARD HOPPER

* estate = la totalité de sa production à sa mort, sauf les œuvres qui font partie des collections privées... si j'ai bien compris.

ET JASPER JOHNS

He really is THE father of pop art, even if most people will say it was Andy Warhol if you ask them, but that's only because <u>your average American</u> is totally ignorant of his own culture...

Ton Américain moyen = Monsieur Tout le Monde

ET PLEIN D'AUTRES...

Quand on a été fatigués de regarder des œuvres d'art, on est allés boire un café et manger un sandwich dans un coffee shop à côté, avant de poursuivre notre éducation (en tout cas celle de Dylan et moi) au Guggenheim.

SOLOMON R. GUGGENHEIM MUSEUM

Solomon R. Guggenheim venait d'une famille qui avait fait fortune grâce à des mines d'or en Alaska. D'après Lizzie, il est difficile d'être plus riche.

I mean like we're talking multi-billionaire type rich, rich like you and me have absolutely no idea!

Mais ce qui m'a le plus impressionnée, c'était le bâtiment lui-même.

This, my friends, is the last ever work of the architectural total genius Frank Lloyd Wright. Now, what we have to do, what Wright intended here, is to take the elevator right to the top and walk slowly down the spiral admiring the works on the way.

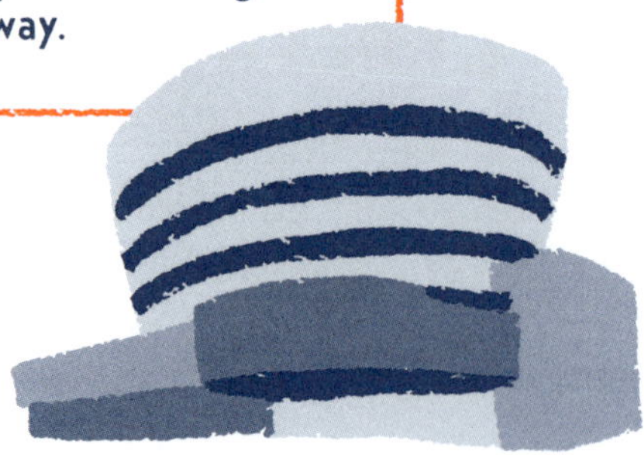

Nous avons donc pris l'ascenseur jusqu'en haut et avons visité le musée en redescendant la spirale de haut en bas. From top to bottom.

Il y avait une exposition consacrée à Josef Albers qui montrait l'évolution de son regard de photographe.

You'll see, Callie, at NYSVA they encourage you to take photos all the time.

Dylan, hearing this, adopted a New York Gangsta pose.

Go on, Callie, take my photo.

Not that sort of photo Dylan. Photos of light, of shadows, of forms.

À partir de là, j'ai commencé à chercher des choses à photographier ; des lumières, des ombres, des formes...

What they say at NYSVA is you have to see things you don't normally notice. How light changes surfaces. How colors change. How space is made through shadows.

J'ai pris des photos de couleurs et de surfaces, d'espaces créés par des ombres (et de Dylan qui n'arrêtait pas de prendre des poses d'idiot chaque fois que je sortais mon appareil photo). J'étais parfaitement heureuse, je voyais déjà le monde d'un œil différent quand... Tout d'un coup un autre visage s'est inséré dans le cadre à côté de celui de Dylan.

C'ÉTAIT ELLE. ENCORE ELLE.

Hey Dylan! Aren't you the lucky one! An Au Pair that takes photos! See you around, kid.

Lizzie looked at me.

Did she just call you an Au Pair?

Et là, dans ma tête...

AU PAIR GIRLS ARE WONDERFUL PEOPLE

Au Pair girls are not just girls

I LOVE BEING AN AU PAIR

WHAT ABOUT AU PAIR BOYS?

IT'S A WAY TO TRAVEL AND LEARN LANGUAGES

AU PAIR GIRLS HELP OVERWORKED MOTHERS

I'M PROUD TO BE AN ALMOST AU PAIR

I'M NOT AN AU PAIR BUT I WISH I WAS

I WISH I WAS AN AU PAIR GIRL

AU PAIRS ARE THE BEST

MY DREAM IS TO BE AN AU PAIR

THURSDAY 30TH AUGUST

BACK TO SCHOOL

Today, we are going shopping with Dylan for his « back to school » stuff.
Aux États-Unis, la rentrée se dit « back to school », retour à l'école, quoi. Et le mot « école » englobe tout, de la maternelle jusqu'au lycée. L'université se dit « college ». Parfois, on précise « high school » pour désigner le lycée, mais pas systématiquement. En général, c'est juste « school ». Cette année, Dylan entre au collège (middle school, 6th grade). Il fait le malin, mais je vois bien qu'il est un peu stressé.
So... Diana gave us a list of things to buy and an envelope full of dollars and said: « That should be enough. Don't buy anything too expensive, but don't buy the really cheap stuff either because it's usually made in China and doesn't last. »

« Enough » :
pronounced « innaff » and means « assez »
(en gros Diana disait que ça devrait suffire)

COMME :

« Have you had enough to eat? »
= as-tu eu assez à manger

OU « That's enough! »
= Ça suffit !

BACK AFTER SHOPPING

SHOPPING WITH DYLAN

Dylan having bought everything, we were coming out of the shop **WHEN...**

Cilla!! My nightmare!!

Hi Dylan! Taking your Au Pair shopping, are you?

She's not my Au Pair, her name's Callie, she's a friend of my parents.

I'm not his Au Pair, my name's Callie, I'm a friend of the family.

Elle m'a toisée de la tête aux pieds aller-retour avant de murmurer : « Yeah, sure » d'un ton pas du tout convaincu et de s'éloigner avec un « See you around, Dylan! », auquel Dylan n'a pas répondu. I looked at Dylan, shaking my head. He shook his head too. Then he said:

You know, a woman like you/should be at home/That's where you belong.

What ??

Bob Dylan. Song called *Sweetheart Like You*.

J'avais oublié cette manie de Dylan et son frère de parler rien qu'avec les paroles des chansons de Bob Dylan qu'ils connaissent par cœur depuis leur enfance. Ils appellent ça « Dylanese », et ça leur permet de dire des choses compliquées avec une langue poétique. Sauf que parfois, c'est tellement poétique que je ne comprends rien. Mais je sentais que Dylan compatissait. J'ai cherché les paroles sur Internet. Je me dis que si je les recopie je finirai peut-être par comprendre quelque chose.

Well the pressure's down, the boss ain't here
He's gone North, for a while
They say that vanity got the best of him
But he sure left here in style
By the way, that's a cute hat
And that smile's so hard to resist
But what's a sweetheart like you doing in a dump like this?

MESSAGE FROM LIZZIE

Want to check out the New Museum for Contemporary Art? I haven't been to the new exhibitions yet.

Yes, sure. When?

In an hour's time?

Perfect. C U there.

Dylan said he'd stay at home, so I'm going to the New Museum with a map so I don't get lost!

THE NEW MUSEUM FOR CONTEMPORARY ART

Les expositions sont ULTRA modernes. Installations, vidéos, performances…
I really like the Sara Magenheimer exhibition entitled NOON, and her text entitled: *Notes on Art and Resistance A - Z*. Here's one entry, letter G: ‹‹ Self-reflection is important. Know your truth. Self-doubt and self-hate serve your oppressor.››

En sortant, je n'ai pas pu m'empêcher de la chercher des yeux. Et de la trouver. Immobile, debout sur le trottoir de l'autre côté de la route. Elle nous fixait, mais comme Dylan n'était pas avec nous, elle ne s'est pas avancée.

Lizzie l'a remarquée.

Isn't that the girl who was outside the Guggenheim? The one that came up to your table in the Minetta Tavern?

What's her problem?

Good question. She's Dylan's brother's girl friend but...

I don't know. She's strange. It's like she's following me. And she calls me Dylan's Au Pair.

Funny... I get the feeling I know her from somewhere...

but I can't remember where...

If she's really following you, you should tell Dylan's parents. It's not cool.

It's weird. I mean, it's sort of not normal.

Si j'étais à la place de Lizzie je me serais sans doute aussi conseillé d'en parler aux parents de Dylan. Mais là... J'ai peur de passer pour une folle. Cela dit, si j'y réfléchis, ça commence à faire beaucoup trop de rencontres pour que ce soit le hasard...

1	Minetta Tavern	→ **OK, Allen brought her with him this time.**
2	In the art supplies shop	→ **Perhaps she studies art too and was shopping for stuff.**
3	Outside Guggenheim's	→ **Perhaps she was about to go and visit the museum.**
4	Outside the shop where we got stuff for school	→ **This is where it gets strange.**
5	Opposite the New Museum	→ **This was creepy (= scary), she just looked at me.**

OK, so this is NOT coincidence. Lizzie is right, it's WEIRD (strange, uncomfortable, disturbing...)

What is also weird is the things she says:

- She calls me the Au Pair,
- She asks if I speak English,
- She says Dylan's taking me for a walk (like I'm a dog...).

BACK HOME

Diana and Frank are in the kitchen. What shall I say? ‹‹ Hi Diana, Frank... Can I talk to you about something? It's probably nothing, but it's a bit weird, and I'm a bit worried (inquiète), scared (effrayée), freaked out (franchement flippée). It's Allen's girl friend... ››

OK HERE I GO... I'M GONE.

I was right to follow Lizzie's advice. Diana and Frank think it's weird too, even if Frank added:

Frank

But it's probably nothing to worry about, just some kid's idea of a joke...

Du coup, ils ont parlé d'Allen et de son « announcement ».

Frank

He's just provoking us, as usual.

Diana

He can't be serious about marrying the girl.

Frank

Yes, well, I think the best thing to do is to not react. Just let it blow over*.

Diana

If only he'd just grow up.

* Let it blow over, laisse-le passer avec le vent (blowing in the wind), c'est ce genre d'idée, comme une tempête qui s'essouffle, je crois. Une métaphore météorologique.

Mais malgré leur discours rassurant, Frank et Diana n'ont pas l'air tranquilles non plus. Diana veut que son fils grandisse : (grow up, un de ces fameux verbes à préposition qui combine le verbe « to grow », pousser, avec la préposition « up », en haut, et qui signifie donc grandir (pousser en hauteur) ou devenir adulte.

FRIDAY 31ST AUGUST

The weather is perfect. Warm and sunny.
At breakfast, Dylan is singing. He's happy and he makes me happy too.
Suddenly I get a text message from Lizzie:

Do U want 2 visit the Met?

Met = Metropolitan Museum.
One of the most famous museums in New York.
More art.

Yes, sure. When?

Noon? Meet U outside.

Noon, c'est midi.
Il est onze heures.

I call Dylan who's playing a video game.

Hey, Dylan, Lizzie's meeting us at the Met.

Cool. When?

Now!

When we arrived at the Met, Lizzie was waiting.
She said: ‹‹ I have some important information for you. ››

LIZZIE'S IMPORTANT INFORMATION

Cilla is a homeless person. She has to sleep in shelters for homeless people.

shelter = abri

HOW DOES LIZZIE KNOW THIS?

Comment elle le sait ?

LIZZIE'S STORY (2)

Where I grew up, there were a lot of homeless people, and, also, shelters for homeless people, and sometimes we'd get food from the shelters. And now I remember where I've seen Cilla before. In the shelters. I remember seeing her a lot, so she must be homeless for a long time...

Je ne me souviens même pas du Met, tellement j'étais concentrée sur les explications de Lizzie et les réactions de Dylan.

DYLAN'S REACTIONS

Dylan

Wow, that's really sad. So that's why she's been following us everywhere. Because she's got no home, no job... she's got nothing to do... Wow. I feel really sorry for her now, even if she is weird.

Me

Yes but why? Why does she follow us?

Lizzie

Because she's jealous of you and scared that Allen might like you better than he likes her.

Pause où je regarde Lizzie en faisant une tête de merlan frit.

Lizzie

Don't look at me like that. You're this brilliant French girl coming to study art in New York. Allen must have told her about you, and she's jealous. Maybe she hasn't even told him she's homeless. Maybe she's scared he won't marry her if he knows.

Well, yes. Homeless people are ashamed of being homeless. If you're homeless, it means you're a failure. You're not a normal member of society. So you don't say anything. You keep it secret.

être un échec

avoir honte

to be ashamed of something

to be a failure

to be hungry

to be cold

(en gros, tout ce qui concerne l'état se dit avec le verbe être en anglais alors qu'en français on utilise aussi le verbe avoir : avoir faim, avoir froid...)

So what shall we do? To make her stop following me everywhere?

WHAT SHALL WE DO?
QU'ALLONS-NOUS FAIRE?

LIZZIE'S SUGGESTION:

Let's talk to Cilla. When you're homeless, you feel like you're invisible. Maybe she just wants you to notice her, Callie.

DYLAN'S SUGGESTION:

Let's talk to Allen. I mean, he's the one who started all this. And he should be told what she's doing, right?

MY SUGGESTION:

Let's just wait. Do nothing yet.
I don't want Allen's girl friend
to be my enemy.

J'ai gagné, sans doute parce que ma solution était la plus simple.

En quittant le Met, on regarde un peu partout à la recherche de Cilla, mais évidemment, maintenant qu'on aimerait presque lui parler, elle n'est pas là. No sign of Cilla anywhere.

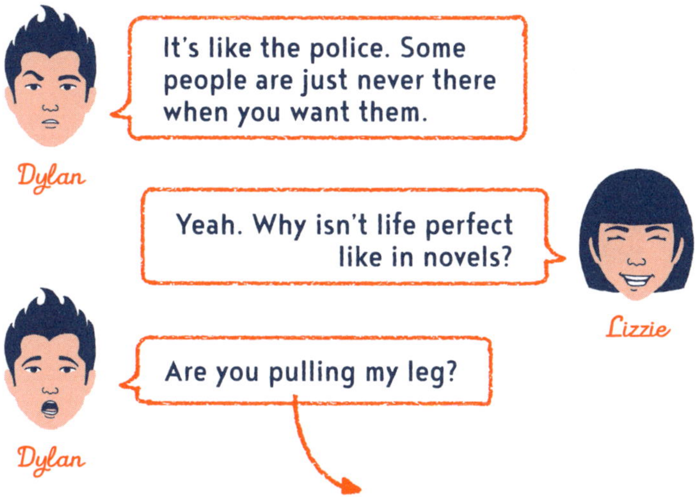

???? EST-CE QUE LIZZIE LUI TIRE LA JAMBE ????

NON, nouvelle expression à noter :

To pull someone's leg =

to make fun of somebody =

se moquer de quelqu'un

SATURDAY 1ST SEPTEMBER

Breakfast. Diana had bought pancakes to heat in the microwave (« réchauffer » se dit juste « to heat »).

Suddenly, Frank said:

Why don't we all take Callie to Ellis Island? After all, she's an immigrant, she should see what it was like before!

Je dois de nouveau ressembler à un merlan frit parce que Diana me vient en aide.

Ellis Island was the first stop for immigrants wanting to enter the United States. There's a museum and a visitor center. Yes, that's a great idea.

Let's go!

Je dois avouer que je suis plutôt soulagée. Je ne pense pas que Cilla osera venir m'embêter devant les parents d'Allen. Et nous partons donc pour Ellis Island...

EVENING

I'm exhausted, but I'll try to write what I remember of our trip.

ELLIS ISLAND

C'est par cette île à l'entrée de New York que sont passés environ 12 millions d'immigrés venus tenter leur chance dans le Nouveau Monde.
Ellis Island became an immigration center in 1892 and closed in 1954. The descendants of the 12 million immigrants who passed through the immigration center now account for almost half the population of the United States of America.

People who arrived through Ellis Island are the ancestors of half the American population today.

Ellis Island was primarily an immigration centre for poor people. Rich people could immediately go to their friends or family.

Ça m'a fait penser au film *Titanic* de James Cameron, où on voyait bien que les conditions du voyage étaient très différentes entre les pauvres et les riches.

Poor people spent two weeks being seasick in horrible conditions, and when they arrived they had a medical and legal inspection.

Since many poor people arrived sick, Ellis Island also had hospital buildings and dormitories for poor people with nowhere to sleep.

FREE BEDS!

Many immigrants arrived with only the clothes they were wearing. They had no money, no food, so there were also kitchens to feed all these people.

FREE FOOD DAILY!

Only 2% of immigrants were refused entry. They were refused for two reasons.

1. If they had a contagious disease.

2. If they were suspected of being an illegal contract labourer.

NO DISEASES. NO ILLEGAL WORKERS.

In 1882, the Chinese Exclusion Act prohibited the immigration of Chinese labourers. This really racist law lasted till 1943.

NO CHINESE

After Ellis Island, we visited the Statue of Liberty. The tourist leaflet says: ‹‹ Its name is Liberty Enlightening the World. ››

torch symbolising the path to liberty

halo showing Liberty is divine

eyes looking out to sea to welcome new immigrants

tablet of law representing July 4th 1776 and the creation of the United States of America

broken chains showing freedom from oppression

Block on which the statue stands built by freemasons

Really cool day.

I COULD ALMOST FORGET CILLA.

SUNDAY 2ND SEPTEMBER

Sue Ann called this morning.

She invited me to lunch to tell me about her project. Sue Ann Vandenberg is a VERY RICH art collector. She has a VERY BIG house in Manhattan. Now she wants to transform part of her house into an exhibition center. She wants me to help. I said yes, of course.

Sue Ann Vandenberg

MONDAY 3RD SEPTEMBER

THIS IS IT!! BACK TO SCHOOL FOR DYLAN AND ME!!

Dylan has left for school wearing his new jeans, his new hoodie, his new trainers and his new backpack. I have packed in my bag all my new stuff. I'm ready for my first day. My first lesson will be English literature with Greg Lipsky, then Economics with Rachel Tan and Sketching with Marina Sørensen. Lizzie will wait for me outside the main entrance.

I'M SOOOO NERVOUS.

backpack

I'M TERRIFIED!

NO, CALLIE, DON'T WORRY, YOU'LL BE FINE.

trainers

hoodie

RIGHT. HERE I GO!

EVENING

I'M TOTALLY EXHAUSTED!

First, we had GREG LIPSKY from nine to ten thirty...

Words are images.

Literature is a magical journey into a world of sensations.

I would like you to READ this description and DRAW what you see.

But also, I would like you to read this description and draw what you FEEL.

For a path seldom* used, its black gravel was miraculously clean of fallen leaves or intruding plant life. About them the trees dripped the second-hand rain of last night's storm onto fern fronds already burdened with crystal drops. (*Ship of Magic*, Robin Hobb, 1998, page 7).

Je n'ai rien compris, ma voisine m'a aidée et...

*Seldom = rarely

THIS IS WHAT I DREW:

Storm = orage

Drip = goutte

Economics class with RACHEL TAN from ten thirty to twelve.

Economics is the science of the production, distribution and consumption of goods and services.

Goods and services are produced and exchanged for money.

Economics means maximum money for minimum effort.

The better the design, the more money will be made.

Design IS economics.

Rachel Tan

TOUT D'UN COUP, JE DÉPRIME...

LUNCH TIME

J'avais à peine franchi le seuil de la porte pour quitter (sans regrets) le cours d'économie quand Lizzie m'a sauté dessus.

Callie, come quick, I've found something you have to see.

I followed her outside. She was walking really quickly.

I just KNEW I'd seen her around here.

We turned a corner onto another street.

I know I've seen her in homeless shelters too, but look!

On the other side of the street, a girl with a guitar was singing outside a coffee shop. **THE GIRL WAS CILLA.**

Mothers and fathers throughout the land, Don't criticise what you can't understand
Joe's Café
JOE'S CAFÉ
Cilla singing Bob Dylan
Waiter with drinks
People having lunch
Hat for money on sidewalk
She's busking, you know, singing on the street and asking people for money.
Lizzie
TO BUSK = faire la manche

J'ai fixé Cilla un bon moment en essayant de comprendre. Lizzie me tirait le bras.

Come on! Let's go and talk to her.

No. She's working.

Elle travaillait, et moi, j'avais besoin de réfléchir. J'ai demandé à Lizzie :

Tell me again, Lizzie... how exactly did you know Cilla was homeless? What were you really doing in the shelters for homeless people?

Parce que Lizzie m'avait donné deux versions différentes de son enfance, et quelque chose clochait...

Lizzie turned red.
Lizzie turned white.
Lizzie had tears in her eyes.

It's OK. I'm your friend.
I don't care if you're homeless.

NOBODY MUST KNOW

Lizzie says.

NOBODY MUST KNOW, BECAUSE...

If they know at work... I'll lose my job. If they know at school... I'll have to leave. If they know at the bank... I'll lose my student loan.

SO.... NOBODY MUST KNOW!

LIZZIE'S STORY (3)

OK, so forget what I told you before, okay. In fact, my parents were sort of into drugs, so I had to be independent and take care of myself, and then my mum died from an overdose when I was about twelve and it was just dad and me, and then dad got AIDS and... well... at sixteen I had to decide. Either the social services and a foster home (host family) or go it alone, and you read so many horrible stories about foster homes, so I decided I'd go it alone. But you know, I was lucky because I'd always been good at school, and that is the one thing that saved me...

J'avais du mal à l'imaginer. Tu perds ta mère à douze ans, ton père tombe malade et meurt lui aussi et à seize ans Lizzie vivait dans la rue ? Et elle avait réussi non seulement à finir le lycée et obtenir son bac, mais aussi à intégrer l'une des écoles d'art les plus prestigieuses de New York ? Seule ?

LIZZIE'S STORY (4)

I really made it thanks to my teachers. They were wonderful. They encouraged me to find solutions. Refuge shelters, their homes from time to time, friends' flats when they went away on holiday... But mainly I was in shelters. That's where I've seen Cilla. She's been on the streets for a while now, because I've been sleeping in shelters for the past year... So what do you want to do?

I WANT TO THINK.

I thought in the sketching lesson. We had a live model to sketch, a real girl. The teacher said:

make your lines nice and round

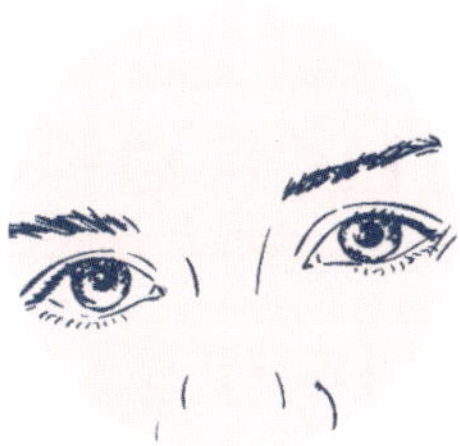

arch the eyebrows

look at the nose

look how the lips are closed

make the eyes alive

I thought while I was walking home.

I thought while I was eating pizza in the kitchen.

I thought while I was watching Dylan play a video game.

Tomorrow morning, I know what I'm going to do. I'm going to be NICE.

NOW I'M GOING TO SLEEP.

TUESDAY 4TH SEPTEMBER

This morning, the lessons were all SCIENTIFIC → Computer science / Color science

LA COULEUR EST DONC UNE SCIENCE !

THE SCIENCE OF COLOR:

VISION = LIGHT → **COLOR IS COMPLICATED.**

of different wavelengths + surface colors that absorb or reflect light + shadows...

J'avais un mal fou à me concentrer.
At ten thirty I texted Lizzie:

Can U meet me 4 lunch?

She answered:

I don't have much time.

I texted back:

I've got an idea. Please.

She answered:

OK

YESSS!!

SOME OF THE THINGS I THOUGHT ABOUT YESTERDAY

WHY IS CILLA SO AGGRESSIVE???

PEOPLE ARE AGGRESSIVE BECAUSE THEY ARE SCARED. FEAR MAKES PEOPLE AGGRESSIVE.

TO BE SCARED = AVOIR PEUR
FEAR = LA PEUR

What do aggressive people fear? What does Cilla fear? What does everybody fear? What do I fear?

FAILURE

FAILURE IS SCARY
(l'échec fait peur)

REASON

FEAR OF FAILURE

I'm scared of failing
I fear failure
I'm aggressive

SO...

I WON'T FAIL

Jusqu'ici tout va bien. MAIS... Comment rester positif face à l'agression de quelqu'un qui a peur ?

DON'T BE AGGRESSIVE TOO

DON'T BE NASTY TOO

DON'T BE ANGRY TOO

BE NICE!

Be nice as ice-cream

BE KIND!

HOW?

HOW DO I STOP ALL THIS AGGRESSIVITY???

I MUST

1. Be **NICE** to Cilla
2. Be **KIND** to Cilla
3. Be **GENEROUS** to Cilla

À midi, j'ai donc entraîné Lizzie en direction du *Joe's café*.

Come on. I'll buy you an ice-cream.

An ice-cream? For lunch?

Yes! We must be nice as ice-cream.

Lizzie m'a regardée comme si j'étais complètement folle.

Come on!

I insisted.

We went to the ice-cream parlour on the corner of the street and I ordered:

THREE GIANT PINK ICE-CREAMS, PLEASE.

I gave one giant pink ice-cream to Lizzie. I crossed the road. I gave one giant pink ice-cream to Cilla.

I said:

Hi, I'm Callie. This is for you, because you sing so beautifully.

I started to eat my giant pink ice-cream.

CILLA THINKS I'M MAD TOO !!

BUT
Cilla starts eating the giant pink ice-cream.

Me

It's like a Buff Monster ice-cream.

Famous street artist

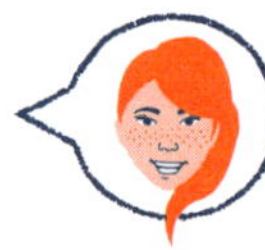

It's good for my throat. Helps me to sing.

Cilla

It's also a peace offering. I want to be your friend.

Why?

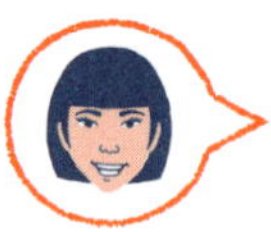

Because it's not good to have enemies. And I like you. You sing really well.

How can you be so NICE??

Well... sometimes it is difficult... but... if you decide to be nice, you just keep being nice, whatever happens...

Lizzie came to join us.

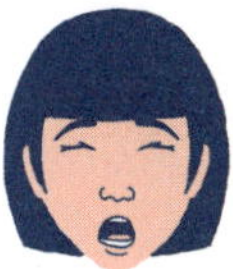

Lizzie

That's what Callie does, she said. She's nice. She's kind. She's generous. She wants to help people. It makes me sick, but there you go...

It makes you sick?

Cilla

She smiled.

Lizzie

Well; you know, nice people... they do make you a bit sick... All that generosity...

I smiled too.

Are you going to vomit all over the sidewalk? Both of you? Because I have an idea.

Me

I'd like you to meet Sue Ann.

They both looked at me. They thought I was mad.

Eh oui. Dimanche, Sue Ann m'avait parlé de son projet, et soudain, j'avais trouvé comment l'aider encore plus…

SUE ANN'S PROPOSAL

I want to create a foundation to help young artists. Young women artists.

I need help from young women artists like you, girls.

I would like you Lizzie and you Cilla to be my two first resident artists.

I have rooms in my house. I will give the rooms to young artists in residency.

Callie has said she'll help me. Will you help me too?

In exchange for a room and a scholarship, you will help me to organise an art gallery and exhibitions in my home.

LIZZIE'S ANSWER:

OK, I mean, thank you, I mean, that would be wonderful, Mrs Vandenberg, I mean, WOW!

CILLA'S ANSWER:

OK on one condition. That Callie will now STOP making everyone's dreams come true and start producing art work.

SUE ANN'S RESPONSE:

You're absolutely right, Cilla. So what if we decide that our first exhibition will be some of Callie's art work? After all, this is a girls' project for women artists, and I think exhibiting the work of a young French artist would attract a lot of people.

ME

WHAT?????

Une expo ?
De mes œuvres ?
Mais je n'en ai pas !

WEDNESDAY 5TH SEPTEMBER

After school today, I collected Dylan from his school and we went to see Sue Ann. Now Cilla and Lizzie live at Sue Ann's house too. Cilla was there. They had spent all afternoon working on the project. Lizzie arrived between the end of school and the start of her job at Minetta Tavern. She had lots of ideas too. Dylan suggested Sue Ann organise days for junior school pupils like him to come and visit exhibitions. We all thought that was a brilliant idea.

Sue Ann said this project was all about

GIRL POWER.

Sue Ann thinks she was LUCKY because her husband was rich and nice. But not all men are rich and nice and girls must learn to be independent. She wants to help young women artists become independent.

SUE ANN'S SPEECH

Did you girls know that 73% of Fine Arts School graduates are girls but only 13% of art works in national and regional collections are from women? Don't you see a problem somewhere? Do girls suddenly lose their creativity when they leave school? NO! But they become dependent.

I WANT TO PROMOTE FEMALE CREATIVITY

BECAUSE

WOMEN ARE STRONG, CREATIVE, IMAGINATIVE

I ALWAYS DREAMED OF BEING AN ARTIST BUT I DIDN'T HAVE THE CONFIDENCE TO TRY

I WANT TO HELP GIRLS BELIEVE IN THEIR CREATIVE POWER

WE ARE GOING TO PROVE TO ALL THOSE GIRLS OUT THERE THAT THEY HAVE VALUE

I WANT GIRLS TO BELIEVE IN THEMSELVES

LATE EVENING

I'm exhausted. I'm so tired! I'm so excited too. It's a wonderful project. A real adventure. And as I was leaving with Dylan (who has to go to bed because he has school tomorrow), Cilla said she wanted to say something.

WHAT I REMEMBER OF WHAT CILLA SAID

Listen, Callie, I'm so sorry I was so aggressive towards you. I don't know why. I wanted Allen to like me, but all he wanted to talk about was you... But honestly, I'm not in love with him. We just said we were going to get married as a joke. Allen wanted to see how you'd react. His parents too. He really likes you, but he's scared, you know. He hardly even knows you, and his parents like you so much he feels he's being forced into a relationship when he doesn't even know if you like him...

THURSDAY 6TH SEPTEMBER

WHAT TO DO ABOUT ALLEN??

* Orgeuil et Préjugés

Spin the hand to decide

LATER. HOME FROM SCHOOL.

This morning, Richard Wilde, our Design as Business teacher, asked us to think about a PROJECT.
He asked us to make a mind map. Here's my mind map for my project for the exhibition at Sue Ann's house:

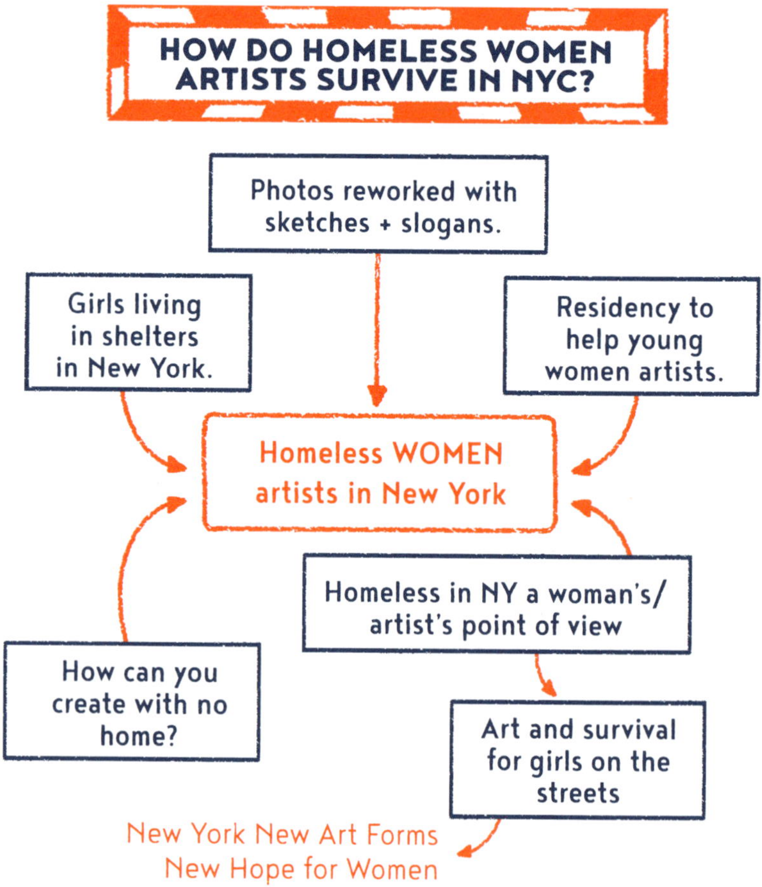

I was really happy when I got out of school... I wanted to hurry and collect Dylan, but...

THIS IS WHAT I SAW

1 Allen waiting for me outside the entrance

eyes glued to the sidewalk

cheeks pink with embarrassment

really unhappy expression

mouth saying « sorry... bad joke... not funny »

2 A van honking its horn as it drove past the entrance

HONK! HONK!!

The *Whole Van* was painted pink!!

What did I do? I just laughed. I don't know why, but it was suddenly so funny. Allen murmuring and looking embarrassed and this painted pink van honking its horn and people looking at it with amazement, it was just so funny. Allen looked at me and relaxed a bit.

HONK!

HONK!!

Do you forgive me then?

No. I will never, ever forgive you.

He looked at me and said:

You're right. It was stupid. So... let's go back in time. It's...

(He looked at his smartphone.)

Monday 27th August and we're at the airport...

MONDAY 27TH AUGUST

At JFK airport (even if we were really on the sidewalk outside NYSVA).

POST-SCRIPTUM → AFTERWARDS WRITTEN

I HATE HAPPY ENDINGS

THIS IS NOT A HAPPY ENDING

THIS IS NOT EVEN AN ENDING

LIFE GOES ON AND YOU CAN'T GO BACK IN TIME.

BUT YOU CAN ALWAYS LOOK ON THE BRIGHT SIDE.

I MUST NOW

- [ ] Finish school
- [ ] Help Sue Ann
- [ ] Become fluent in English
- [ ] Find a job
- [ ] Be happy with the Gardners
- [ ] Prepare an exhibition for Sue Ann...

AND ALLEN???

TO BE CONTINUED...

L'AUTRICE

Stéphanie Benson est née à Londres en 1959. Arrivée en France en 1981, elle publie son premier roman pour adultes en 1995, puis se lance dans le roman policier jeunesse aux éditions Syros (*L'Inconnue dans la maison*, *La Disparue de la 6e B*, *Une Épine dans le pied*, *Shooting Star*...). Aujourd'hui autrice de plus de cinquante romans pour petits et grands (dont la série *Epicur* au Seuil), elle écrit également des nouvelles, de la poésie, ainsi que des pièces de théâtre dont des pièces radiophoniques pour France Inter et France Culture, et des scénarios pour la télévision. Parallèlement à sa vie d'autrice, elle est maître de conférences en anglais et didactique à l'université Bordeaux-Montaigne.

Crédits photos :

· Page 79 :

– Immigrants refused admission to the United States awaiting their return passage, Ellis Island, c.1902.
© Shutterstock/ Everett Historical

– Old immigrants baggage at the Ellis Island Museum on January 21, 2010 in New York. Ellis Island, the gateway for immigrants to USA, was immigrant inspection station from 1892 to 1954.
© Shutterstock/ Chirajuti

· Page 80 :

– Women immigrants undegoing a physical examination, Ellis Island, New York, ca. November 1910.
© Shutterstock/ Everett Historical

– Directional sign marking the way to Chinatown and Little Italy in Manhattan, New-York.
© Shutterstock/ Elbud

· Page 81 :

– The Statue of Liberty in New York City
© Shutterstock/ NaughtyNut

· Page 93 :

– Portrait of beautiful young girl, Vector sketch, Hand drawn illustration
© Shutterstock/ Art of line

Achevé d'imprimer en janvier 2019
par Pollina (85400 Luçon, France) - 87359

IMPRIM'VERT
Votre imprimeur agit pour l'environnement

FSC
www.fsc.org
MIXTE
Papier issu de
sources responsables
FSC® C022030